CW00841347

THIS WALKER BOOK BELONGS TO:

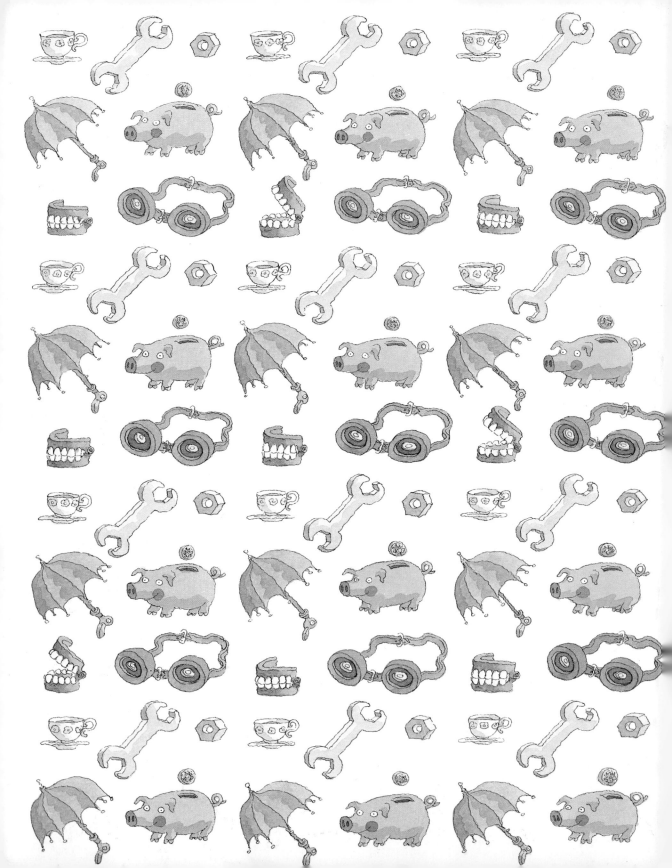

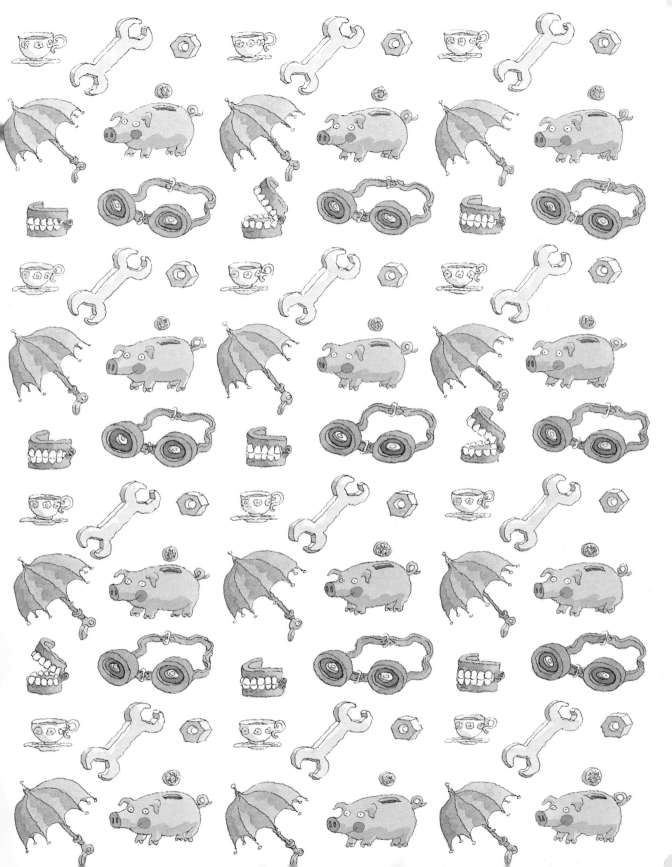

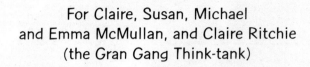

For Claire, Susan, Michael
and Emma McMullan, and Claire Ritchie
(the Gran Gang Think-tank)

M.W.

For Auntie Bill

D.M.

First published 1988 by
Walker Books Ltd
87 Vauxhall Walk
London SE11 5HJ

First printed 1988
Printed in Hong Kong by Sheck Wah Tong Printing Press Ltd

British Library Cataloguing in Publication Data
Waddell, Martin
Great Gran Gorilla and the robbers.
I. Title   II. Mansell, Dom
823'. 914 [J] PZ7

ISBN 0-7445-0751-0
ISBN 0-7445-0753-7 pbk

GREAT GRAN GORILLA
GORILLA
and the Robbers

Written by

MARTIN WADDELL

Illustrated by

DOM MANSELL

WALKER BOOKS

LONDON

DO NOT CYCLE
ON THE GRASS

DO NOT PADDLE

DO NOT FEED
THE DUCKS

BY ORDER.

One day the Gran Gang were at their
H.Q. in the Park. Gran Brown was feeding
the ducks. Gran Jones was paddling.
Gran Smith was looking beautiful.
Great Gran Gorilla was doing super-
wheelies. A special message came through
on Gran Brown's hearing aid.

 "Go at once to Green Street! Robbers!"
was the message.

The Gran Gang

R RR RROOOAARRED into action.

This is the Gran Gang roaring down

the Main Street.

Here are the robbers. They are big and fierce.

They go around punching and stealing.

Here comes the Gran Gang.
Peeep! Peeeep! Peeeeep!

Robbers are flying everywhere!
Grans are flying too!

"Surrender!" cried Great Gran Gorilla.
"Not to a load of old ladies!" cried the

Robbers' Boss, gnashing his teeth.

"Get them, girls!" cried Great Gran Gorilla.

Gran Smith and Gran Jones and Gran
Brown attacked with their umbrellas.

Great Gran Gorilla is chasing the Robbers' Boss.
The Robbers' Boss is very big and strong but...
GREAT GRAN GORILLA IS BIGGER!

Great Gran Gorilla got him!

The three robbers are tied up in the lasso.

Great Gran Gorilla is sitting on the Robbers' Boss.

"Oh, well done, Grans!" cried all the people, and they gave the Grans lots of presents.

This is the Grans back at their Granny Flat enjoying their presents.

Gran Smith has the potted plant and Gran Jones has the knitted cardigan and Gran Brown has the strawberry jam.

Great Gran Gorilla got the Iron Bar Bending Kit. They all had crumpets for tea, dipped in beer. Then they got ready for bed.

Gran Smith put Ginger out.

Gran Brown put Tiddles out.

Gran Jones put Goliath out.

Great Gran Gorilla put Fluffy out.

They all went to bed.

Gran Smith and Gran Jones and Gran Brown
dreamt about being Dear Old Ladies.

But Great Gran Gorilla dreamt about...
THE GRAN GANG'S NEXT ADVENTURE!

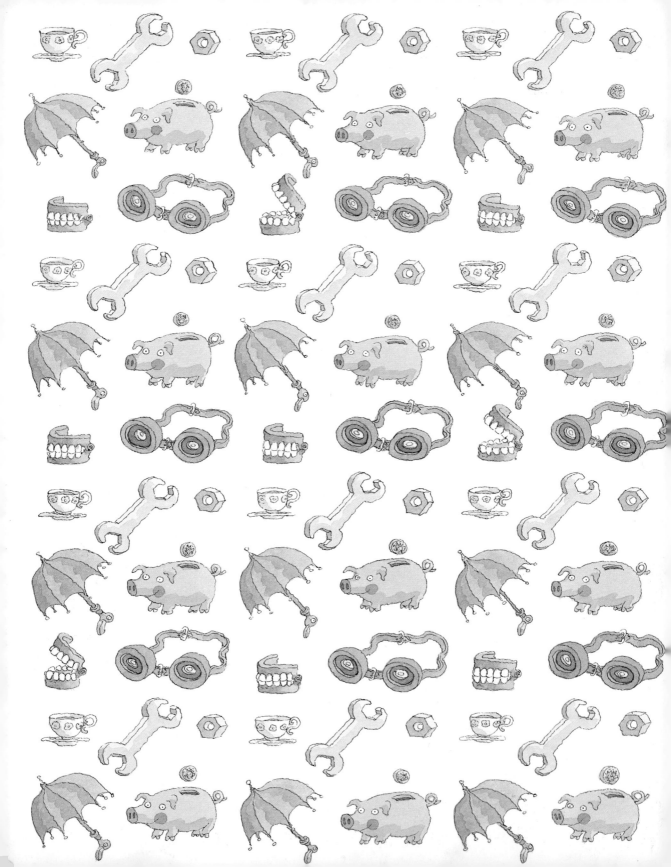

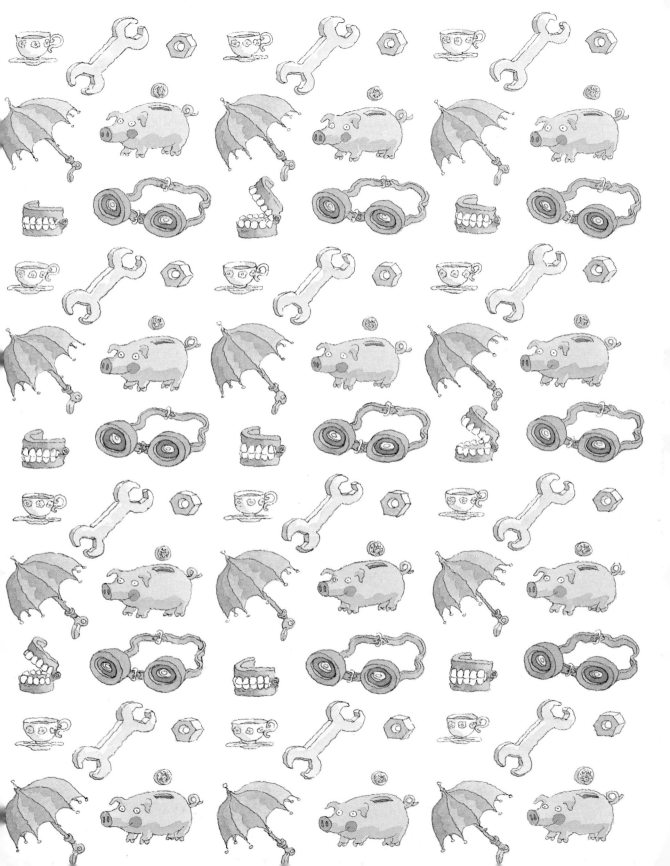

MORE WALKER PAPERBACKS

PICTURE BOOKS
For 4 to 6-Year-Olds

Sarah Hayes
The Walker Fairy Tale Library
BOOKS ONE TO SIX
Six collections of favourite stories

Helen Craig
Susie and Alfred
THE NIGHT OF THE PAPER BAG MONSTERS
A WELCOME FOR ANNIE

Jane Asher & Gerald Scarfe
The Moppy Stories
MOPPY IS HAPPY   MOPPY IS ANGRY

PICTURE BOOKS
For 6 to 10-Year-Olds

Martin Waddell
& Joseph Wright
Little Dracula
LITTLE DRACULA'S FIRST BITE
LITTLE DRACULA'S CHRISTMAS
LITTLE DRACULA AT THE SEASIDE
LITTLE DRACULA GOES TO SCHOOL

Patrick Burston
& Alastair Graham
Which Way?
THE PLANET OF TERROR
THE JUNGLE OF PERIL

E.J. Taylor
Biscuit, Buttons and Pickles
IVY COTTAGE   GOOSE EGGS

Quentin Blake
& Michael Rosen
Scrapbooks
UNDER THE BED
HARD-BOILED LEGS
SMELLY JELLY SMELLY FISH
SPOLLYOLLYDIDDLYTIDDLYITIS

Peter Dallas-Smith
& Peter Cross
TROUBLE FOR TRUMPETS

Adrian Mitchell
& Patrick Benson
THE BARON RIDES OUT

David Lloyd
& Charlotte Voake
THE RIDICULOUS STORY OF
GAMMER GURTON'S NEEDLE

Selina Hastings
& Juan Wijngaard
SIR GAWAIN AND THE LOATHLY LADY